To moms and dads,
especially George and Nancy, Meg and Stan

First U.S. Edition

Library of Congress Cataloging in Publication Data
Butterworth, Nick.
    The Nativity Play.

    Summary: Sam and his sister join their classmates in putting on a school nativity play, appearing as shepherds, animals, and wise men to tell the story of the birth of Christ.
    (1. Christmas–Fiction. 2. Jesus Christ–Nativity–Fiction. 3. Plays–Fiction) I. Inkpen, Mick.
II. TITLE.
PZ7.B98225NAT   1985   (E)   85-10432
ISBN 0-316-11903-2

Printed in Belgium by Henri Proost + Cie, Turnhout

THE NATIVITY PLAY

NICK BUTTERWORTH AND MICK INKPEN

Little, Brown and Company

Boston   Toronto

Tracy and Sam are in their school nativity play.
Their mom is helping with the costumes.
Tracy is one of the angels. She feels beautiful in her
golden halo. She wants a magic wand.
But Mom says that angels don't have magic wands.

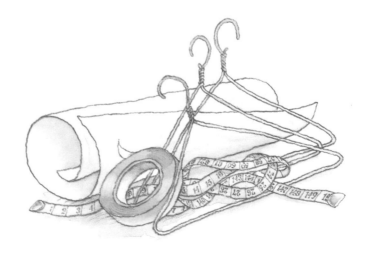

Sam is a shepherd. With enough striped towels
he'll look just like the real thing.
Mom is having trouble with his beard. It's made
of wool and Scotch tape, but it won't stay on.
Sam is practicing his words. "The Savior of
the world is born, the Savior of the world is
born," he says to himself.
"Don't worry," says Mom. "It'll be all right on
the night of the play."

At last everything is ready.
The audience are in their seats. Mom and Dad are
sitting in the front row with Mrs. Booth from next door.
Backstage, everyone is feeling nervous.
"Now," says Miss Harvey, "nice and loud, everybody.
And, shepherds, don't stand in front of Mary."

The curtain opens.
"InthedaysofCaesarAugustus…"
"Slow down a bit, Katie," whispers Miss Harvey.
"Joseph the carpenter and his wife, Mary, went
up to Bethlehem…"

Joseph looks for somewhere to stay.
"No room," says the first innkeeper.
"Full up," says the second innkeeper.
"Too late," says the third innkeeper.
"But I am worried about my wife. She is
having a baby," says Joseph with a grin.
The third innkeeper has an idea.
"I have a stable you can use," he says.

"And so Mary's baby, Jesus, was born in a stable."
The animals gather around the baby. They begin
to sing.
"Away in a manger, no crib for a bed,
The little Lord Jesus lay down his sweet head…"
"Sing out," says Miss Harvey.

Here come the shepherds! But where's Sam?
Ah — it's all right. He was in the bathroom.
Tracy, the beautiful angel, stands in front of them.
"Fear not!" she shouts. "I bring you tidings of great joy."
She tells the shepherds
all about the baby Jesus.
The other angels play
their recorders.

"Come, let us go over to Bethlehem," say the shepherds.
They gather around to look at the baby.
One of the shepherds is looking at the audience.
He waves. "Hello, Dad."

Now comes Sam's big moment. He walks to
the front. His voice is clear and loud.
"The Savior of the world is born," he tells
the audience.
"Lovely," says Mrs. Booth.

There is a noise at the back of the hall.
Wise men are coming from the east. But the
door won't open.
One of the dads lets them in.
Slowly, the wise men walk up to the stage.
They look serious.
Their camel is having trouble climbing the steps.

"Where is he who is born to be king?
For we have seen his star in the east and have
come to worship him," says the wise man
with the bath salts. Joseph points.
The wise men lay their gifts by the manger.
"Gold I give to the infant king."
"Frankincense is the gift I bring."
"Myrrh is mine, so let us sing,
Our joyful Christmas praises ring…"

So Joseph and Mary, the innkeepers,
the shepherds, the angels, the wise men,
the camel, the donkey, the sheep and the cow
all sing together.
"Join in, everybody," says Miss Harvey.
Mr. Bryant, the custodian, switches on the
overhead projector and up come the words.

Hark! the herald angels sing,
Glory to the new-born King,
Peace on earth, and mercy mild,
God and sinners reconciled.
Joyful, all ye nations, rise,
Join the triumph of the skies;
With the angelic host proclaim,
Christ is born in Bethlehem.

PRINTED IN BELGIUM BY
proost
INTERNATIONAL BOOK PRODUCTION